By

Lynne N. Lockhart and Barbara M. Lockhart

Illustrated by Lynne N. Lockhart

Rambling Raft

Tidewater Publishers
Centreville, Maryland

D1275160

One summer morning Mr. Abbott stopped at the Bait and Tackle Shop on River Road. He bought two new crab pots for himself and a new red life jacket for his boy, Scott. Just as he was paying for them, Mr. Abbott noticed a blue and yellow raft leaning against the fishing rods over in one corner of the store.

"That's what I want for my son, Scott," he told the salesman. "Tomorrow's his birthday. He needs this new life jacket because his old one is too small, but I know he'd love that raft!"

Mr. Abbott hung the life jacket in the cab of the pickup, and put the crab pots and the raft in the back of the truck. Chessie, Scott's dog, barked at the raft and wagged his tail as if he knew exactly who it was for.

On the way home, Mr. Abbott discovered a blue heron stalking for a fishy breakfast at the edge of the marsh. He was so interested in the heron, he didn't see the bump in the road.

Bam! went the truck. "Awwwwwwwk" went the heron as he reached out his long snake of a neck and pulled his body up into the air with his wide wings. Mr. Abbott watched, astonished.

In the back of the truck, Chessie slipped, and the
raft went flying high in the air like a big balloon and
bounced into the weeds at the side of the road. But Mr.
Abbott never even noticed.

Not long after, Eddie and Karen came by.

"Hey, look!" they shouted to each other, racing toward the raft.

"Finders keepers!" Karen sang out.

"Grab the other end," Eddie told her. "Let's go down to the beach."

The sun was steamy hot, so the children held the raft upside down over their heads. They looked like a giant blue and yellow turtle making its way down to the sea.

All afternoon they played pirates. They captured rock and shell treasures from the shallow water along the shore where the minnows play. The raft became so heavy with treasures that it began to fill with water.

By the time the pirates got their ship to shore, mothers were calling them to supper. They loaded their T-shirts with their favorite "keepers" and scurried off, leaving the raft to rock gently in the water, nudging the sandy bottom.

Soon a family of ducks paddled by. Just as the smallest duckling (and the last in line) swam close, a wave from a passing boat made the raft tip to one side. The duckling was scooped up and began paddling around in a little pool of his very own. When Mama Duck saw what had happened, she quacked and scolded. With all the other ducklings following her, she swam right into the blue and yellow raft.

Mama preened her feathers and the little ones splashed and dove, flapped their wings and shook their tails until there was very little water left in the raft.

It was time to go. Nudging the ducklings up over the side of the raft, Mama led her babies to the quiet waters of the marsh where they would find their dinner.

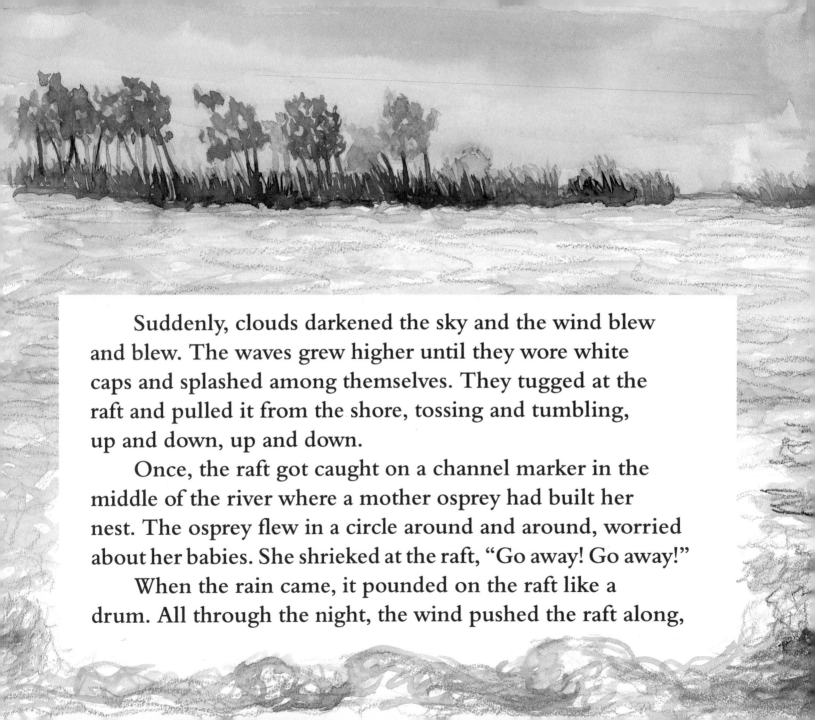

Suddenly, clouds darkened the sky and the wind blew and blew. The waves grew higher until they wore white caps and splashed among themselves. They tugged at the raft and pulled it from the shore, tossing and tumbling, up and down, up and down.

Once, the raft got caught on a channel marker in the middle of the river where a mother osprey had built her nest. The osprey flew in a circle around and around, worried about her babies. She shrieked at the raft, "Go away! Go away!"

When the rain came, it pounded on the raft like a drum. All through the night, the wind pushed the raft along,

but when morning came, the raft had settled upside down
on a pile of reeds and twigs in the marsh that was the home
of the muskrat family. Mother Muskrat was just wondering
what the little ones were chirping about when she saw

the blue and yellow roof like a circus tent covering their
house. The babies turned somersaults and jumped from
each other's shoulders like acrobats until Mother Muskrat
said, "Enough of that!"

Gradually, the tide came in and lifted the raft just
a bit so it could float off on its own again.

This time the raft went past the crab pots which had
been set out that morning. Their bleach-bottle floats bobbed
up and down with the raft. A sailboat breezed by, its rainbow
sails billowing in the wind.

Two sea gulls were flying high above the water, watch-
ing for fish, when they noticed the raft.

"What kind of fish is that?" they seemed to be saying
as they swooped down to investigate.

"Why, it's not a fish at all. It's a special sea gull bed!"
The sea gulls closed their eyes and stood on one leg.

"Ack! Watch out!" squawked one of the gulls as the wake from a cabin cruiser flipped the raft over.

"This is no place for a nap!" said the other gull. With that, the sea gulls flew off, turning and diving as they fished for lunch.

Mr. Abbott had just finished checking his crab pots
and was on his way in when he heard the sea gulls laughing
among themselves and turned to look. And there was
the raft!

"That looks exactly like the one I bought for Scott,"
he said to himself as he steered his workboat toward the
raft.

"Hey, it is! I knew it must have flown out of the truck yesterday. I've been looking everywhere for it. But how did it get out here? It's a good thing I heard those sea gulls," said Mr. Abbott as he tied the raft to the boat, "because today is Scott's birthday."

Scott was waiting on the pier for his father to come home just as he did every day. He was wearing his new birthday present life jacket, ready for the ride in the work-boat his father promised him.

"Got an extra-special catch today!" shouted his father as he pulled in. "Happy birthday, Scott!" he called, towing the raft right up to the pier.

A raft of his own! A real boat! Scott jumped in the raft and it seemed to hug him as it bounced and wobbled, almost dumping him out. Lucky he had his life jacket on! A second later, Chessie jumped in too.

Scott played and paddled all afternoon while his father washed the deck of his boat and the sea gulls flew overhead.

When the boat was ready for tomorrow's catch, Scott tied his raft next to his father's workboat—finders keepers this time for sure.